I will Rejoice

Written by **Karma Wilson**

Illustrated by **Amy June Bates**

zonderkidz

zonder**kidz**
The children's group
of Zondervan

www.zonderkidz.com

I Will Rejoice
Copyright © 2006 by Karma Wilson
Illustrations © 2006 by Amy June Bates

Requests for information should be addressed to:
Grand Rapids, Michigan 49530

ISBN 10: 0-310-71117-7
ISBN 13: 978-0-310-71117-9

Zonderkidz is a trademark of Zondervan.

Published in association with Writer's House.

Illustrations used in this book were created using watercolor.
The body text for this book is set in Century Old Style.

Printed in China

07 08 09 10 • 10 9 8 7 6 5 4 3 2 1

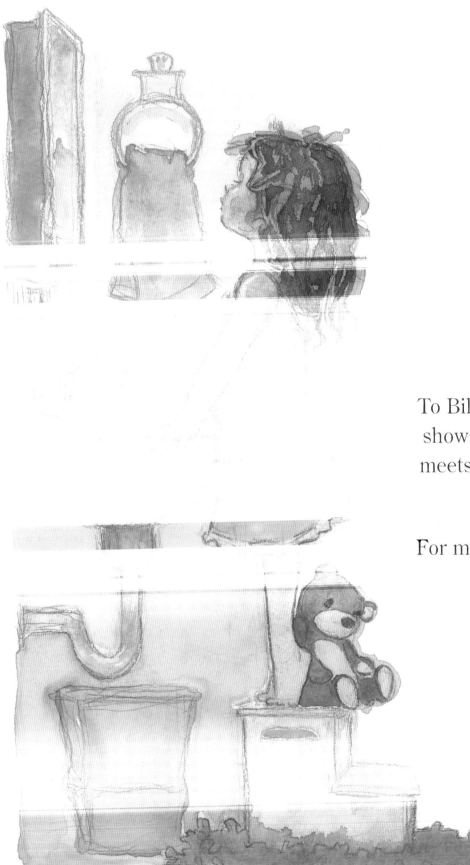

To Bill Donavon, who
shows everybody he
meets how to rejoice.
— K.W.

For my mom and dad.
— A.B.

Celebrating Scripture Psalm 118:24
This is the day the L***ORD has made; let us rejoice and be glad in it.

This is the day that the LORD has made,
and I will rejoice and be glad in it.

I will rejoice in the early light
with a good morning kiss
and a hug so tight.

I'll dress myself up,
sit down in my seat,
and give thanks to the LORD
for the food that I eat.

This is the day that the LORD has made,
and I will rejoice and be glad in it.

I will rejoice as I run and I play.
Thank you, dear God,
for this beautiful day!

I'll sit at the table and eat up my lunch.
(I'll save a few bites for my teddy to munch.)

This is the day that the LORD has made,
and I will rejoice and be glad in it.

I will rejoice in a warm, cozy lap,
as I hear a good story before my noon nap.

I'll lie down and dream
about castles and kings,
princes and dragons
with shimmering wings.

This is the day that the LORD has made,
and I will rejoice and be glad in it.

I will rejoice in the evening light
when my family is home,
settled in for the night.

We'll sit and eat dinner and talk of the day.
Then later we'll laugh as we wrestle and play.
This is the day that the LORD has made,
and I will rejoice and be glad in it.

I will rejoice and get ready for bed.
I'll snuggle down tight and lay down my head.

I'll cuddle up close to my trusty, old bear,
and give thanks for Jesus
as we say our prayer.

I'll get hugs and kisses
from Mom, and then Dad.
And tomorrow again
I'll rejoice and be glad.

DATE DUE

JUL 05 2009